Thunder
on the Plains

Gary Robinson

7th Generation
Summertown, Tennessee

Library of Congress Cataloging-in-Publication Data

Robinson, Gary, 1950-
Thunder on the plains / by Gary Robinson.
    pages cm
  ISBN 978-1-939053-00-8 (pbk. : alk. paper) -- ISBN 978-1-939053-86-2
(e-book : alk. paper) (print)
  1. Cheyenne Indians--Juvenile fiction. I. Title.
  PZ7.R56577Th 2012
  [Fic]--dc23   2012039546

7th Generation, a division of
Book Publishing Company
PO Box 99, Summertown, TN 38483
888-260-8458
bookpubco.com

ISBN: 978-1-939053-00-8

18 17 16 15 14 13   1 2 3 4 5 6 7 8 9

Printed in the United States

Contents

Thunder
on the Plains

Gary Robinson

Chapter 1
The One-Two Punch

I sometimes wonder what goes on in my room before I wake up or when I'm not there. Do my books and CDs move from one place to another so I can't ever find them? Does my soccer ball roll across the floor so I'll trip on it when I come in the door? These are mysteries I may never solve.

The first thing I remember hearing on this particular morning was the opening words of Road Warriors' hit song "Don't Hate Me" blasting at full volume. "Don't hate me 'cause I live on Native land. Don't hate me 'cause I am who I am."

I stuck my arm out from under the covers and searched for the snooze button to quiet the bass drum throbbing in my ears. The pounding stopped.

"Daniel Nathan Wind!" My mother's voice came from down the hall. "You'd better not push that snooze button. You've got to get up and finish your report for school!"

A moan escaped from somewhere deep inside me. Dragging myself upright, I flung the star quilt off me. My grandmother made this quilt for me years ago when I was little. We lived on the reservation then.

I tried to make my eyes focus. The first thing that came into view was the front of my T-shirt. The faded writing shouted "Road Warriors Live On Stage!" That reminded me of their concert I got to go to last year. Awesome!

I looked up at the ceiling above the bed to see the poster I'd taped up there. The guys from Road Warriors glared back at me with painted war faces. Urban skins, just like me.

"Danny! Do you hear me?" my mother called again.

"All right, Mom. All right."

I took a look around my room. Rays of morning sunlight streamed through the window and onto the bed. Was this the typical room of a typical teenager? Dirty clothes covered parts of the floor. The faces of rock stars, skateboarders, and race car drivers looked back at me from the posters that lined my walls.

My "Duty Calls" video game called to me. I had left it on all night. My laptop computer waited in standby mode for me to bring it to life.

First I had to bring my brain to life. I realized it was Monday. My history report was due today. That's what Mom was yelling about. I got up slowly and sat at the desk. Cheese from a slice of uneaten pizza hung over the edge of a bookshelf. Several soda cans stood guard around the pizza like cops guarding an armored truck.

I took a bite of pizza. It was cold. I took a sip of one of the sodas. It was warm. I touched the computer keyboard. The screen woke up a lot faster than I did. The title of my history report showed at the top. "The Civil War in

Indian Territory" was waiting to be written. I began typing.

Fifteen minutes later, I hit the print button and got up to get dressed. The left side of the closet contained clothes approved by my school. My mother had picked out that stuff. The right side held the clothes I wore all other times. Whenever possible. It was a school day. Of course, I had to choose a shirt and pants from the left side. Really stylish.

After dressing, I gathered up the pages from my printer. I stuffed them into my backpack without reading them. I was confident the report would be fine as is.

I stumbled into the kitchen to see what else there was to eat for breakfast. My mother was standing at the stove cooking a batch of scrambled eggs. My stepfather, Bill, was reading a newspaper at the table.

Mom was already dressed for work. A bright red apron covered most of her beige dress. Her dark brown skin and black hair told me she was still Indian underneath. I always liked it better when her daily wear was blue jeans and denim shirts. They seemed more Indian somehow.

"Good morning, sleepyhead," she said.

"Morning," I mumbled.

Mom scraped the eggs onto a plate and set it in front of my stepfather. Bill was a white businessman, forty years old. He was wearing his usual gray suit, white shirt, and blue tie. He was from another world.

"Did you finish that report?" Mom asked me.

"Yeah, it's done."

"Good," my stepfather said. He always seemed angry when he spoke to me. I think Mom said he was "stern," not angry. He folded the newspaper and picked up his fork.

"We wouldn't want a repeat of the problems we had last month, would we?"

I didn't answer.

"Want some eggs and bacon?" Mom asked in a cheerful voice. She was always trying to smooth things over between Bill and me.

I nodded and reached for the pitcher of orange juice. I certainly wished things could be like they used to be. My full-blooded Cheyenne father died in an accident at work two years ago. I'm still not over it. I don't think Mom is either. Really. But she tries to hide her sadness.

It was right after Dad died that my life began to fall apart. For some reason, things just didn't go right any more. School was a hassle. Home life was a hassle. I couldn't stay focused on any one thing. My mind was a mess. How could it be any other way? Dad and I were close.

But then Mom announced a year later that she was going to get married. This white guy named Bill from the bank where she worked asked her to. I couldn't believe it. I wasn't ready for a replacement father in my life. Especially someone as different from me and Mom as Bill is. Mom said he was good to her. She said he would make our lives a lot more stable.

This was way too much for a fourteen-year-old boy to handle. First my dad's gone. Then Mom replaces him with a stranger. Pow! Pow! It hit me in the gut like a one-two punch.

Dad always said I was a pretty smart kid. So why had my grades started dropping? And why was the principal calling me into his office every other week? He'd said I was "acting out," whatever that means.

"You need to eat before your food gets cold," Mom said, putting down the plate in front of me. A smiley face made from two fried eggs and a curled strip of bacon looked up from the plate.

"Wathene, we need to leave in ten minutes," Bill said to my mother.

The food she had cooked tasted good. As I ate, Mom worked my long black hair into a single braid down my back. I pretended not to like it, but secretly I did. It reminded me of when Dad was alive. Mom would braid his hair like this before he went to work.

After breakfast, the three of us got into Bill's car, a shiny new blue Buick. We took our regular route to my school. The busy streets of Los Angeles were crowded with other cars headed to offices and schools. My school, the D. W. Griffith Middle School, was named after some old Hollywood director that I'd never heard of.

Sitting in back of the Buick gave me more time to think about the past. We had moved into Bill's house here in the San Fernando Valley when Mom and Bill got married. It was definitely a high-class house in a high-class neighborhood. Especially when you compared it to our old frame house on the east side of L.A.

Before Bill, we had lived in a mixed neighborhood of African American, Latino, and Native American families. Everyone lived in small homes crammed together. It was sort of like a big tossed salad. Our fancy new neighborhood seemed a lot more like a loaf of bread— white bread.

I dreaded going to school today. And it wasn't just because of the math test in third period. Or the quickly written history report. It was mainly because of Willy Phillips. Willy was the blond-haired bully of Griffith Middle School. He had promised to clean my clock this week. But he wasn't talking about a timepiece. I knew he meant he was going to beat me up.

"Good luck on your math test, dear," Mom said as I got out of the car in front of the school.

"And try to stay out of trouble, okay?" Bill added. "There's only a month and a half left of school. I know you can do it, sport." He winked at me as the car pulled away. I hated being called "sport."

And they didn't know about Willy.

Chapter 2
Moments of Brilliance

By noon I was feeling better about the day. My math test had been easier than I expected. I only had to fake it on a few of the questions. There was a substitute teacher in language arts who showed us a film about William Shakespeare. And in social studies, the teacher told me my Civil War report looked "interesting."

That afternoon I had science and computer lab, my two favorite subjects. So all I had to do was dodge Willy Phillips during lunch. Then I'd be home free.

I found Jesse in the lunchroom and sat down beside him. Jesse is my best friend. He's a Latino boy who likes a lot of the same things I do. We ate lunch together most days. After lunch we would go to science and computer lab together.

"Hey, Jesse, what's for lunch?" He had gotten a tray of cafeteria food. I could tell he was trying to figure out exactly which food group each item was from.

"Today is Monday, so I guess this must be last Wednesday's meatloaf disguised as lasagna," he said, cutting into the food like a surgeon operating on a patient.

I opened my brown paper bag to see what my mother had packed for lunch.

"Boy, have I got a surprise for you," Jesse said in a whisper. He looked around to see if anyone was watching.

"I think the coast is clear," I told him, also whispering. "What are we whispering for?"

Jesse opened a notebook. He took out a piece of paper and slipped it to me.

"With my devilish mind and your computer wizardry, what sort of chaos can we create with this?" he asked.

I looked at the paper. It was a sheet of stationery from the principal's office. It had the school's name, address, and official school seal at the top. The principal's name was printed at the bottom.

"Where did you get this?" I asked.

"I just lifted it from Mr. Rippleton's desk this morning when he wasn't looking."

"What were you doing in the principal's office?" My eyes widened.

"Just clearing up a little dispute about who glued Mrs. Wright's locker shut last week," Jesse said.

"Well, this really isn't much use without Mr. Rippleton's signature."

"Which you have on the note he wrote when you almost got suspended last month."

"Which I happen to have right here!"

I dug around in my backpack. I knew it was in there somewhere. By the time I found it, an idea had hatched in my mind. It was an idea that was perfect for computer lab. Where do these moments of brilliance come from? For some reason, I failed to see the trouble it could cause me.

That afternoon in computer lab I waited for just the right moment. It came while the teacher was busy helping someone with a question. I placed the stationery on the lab's scanner and scanned it into the lab's computer. Then, when the teacher was busy putting a new cartridge in another printer, I scanned the principal's signature into the computer. The final step was to put both files on my flash drive. When this was done, I gave Jesse the thumbs-up sign. We were good to go.

"What's with the thumbs up, Daniel?" the teacher asked. He took me by surprise.

"Are you pretending to be the emperor of Rome? And now you're going to allow the gladiator to live?"

"No, Mr. Saunders." I had to think fast. "Jesse and I had a little bet about who could finish this software problem first. I won." I laughed nervously and glanced at Jesse.

"Oh, I see." I don't think he really believed me. But another student asked a question just then and saved me. I sighed with great relief and held up the flash drive to show Jesse.

When school was out for the day, I had Jesse scout up ahead to see if there was any sign of Willy. After peeking out the front doors, he signaled back that the coast was clear. I bolted for the school bus. My unpleasant meeting with Willy was postponed for at least another day.

I was what they call a "latchkey" kid. I always got home from school before Mom and Bill got home from work, so I had a key to let myself into the house. This gave me plenty of time to complete the day's mission.

I took the flash drive out of my backpack and put it in my computer. Then I copied the two files I'd scanned at school onto my hard drive. Next, I sat down to write the letter I'd been thinking about on the bus.

"Dear Parents and Teachers," the letter began. "I am sorry to announce that school will be closed tomorrow, Wednesday, May 14, due to faulty electrical wiring that was just discovered. This problem must be taken care of as soon as possible so that no one gets hurt. I hope this isn't a problem on such short notice, but it don't really matter. We have to do it anyway."

Then I merged the three documents—the letter, the stationery, and the signature—to create my final masterpiece. This is good, I thought, and emailed a copy to Jesse. I printed out fifty copies of the letter and stuffed them into my school backpack.

The mechanical voice in my computer said, "You've got mail." It was from Jesse.

"You've outdone yourself this time," his message said. "You should be in the hacker's hall of fame. Jesse :-)"

The next morning, Jesse and I secretly passed out the letter among the students. While I distracted the school secretary, Jesse put copies of the letter in the teachers' mailboxes. By noon, the whole school was buzzing with talk of getting a day off.

But, of course, this didn't last long. Just before the lunch bell, Mr. Rippleton came on the school speaker system and announced that school would be open as usual on Wednesday after all.

"I believe I know who the culprit is who started this rumor. He will be dealt with speedily," Mr. Rippleton ended the announcement. Uh-oh.

I was immediately summoned to the principal's office. Mr. Saunders, the computer teacher, was there, too. Mr. Rippleton was furious. He held a copy of letter tightly in his hand. He paced back and forth. He couldn't believe that one of his students could do such a thing.

"I hope this isn't a problem on such short notice, but it don't really matter," he read out loud from the letter.

"In addition to everything else you've done wrong, Mr. Wind, your grammar stinks. It should read 'but it *doesn't* really matter.'" The principal paced some more.

"You've outdone yourself this time, mister," he continued. That sounded better when Jesse said it yesterday. "This is the act of a borderline criminal."

I had to think fast. Again.

"But Mr. Rippleton," I protested, "it was just a class assignment that got out of hand. I didn't know it was going to get passed out all over school."

"Is this true, Mr. Saunders?" the principal asked.

Mr. Saunders look puzzled. I jumped in just as the computer teacher was about to speak.

"You see, the assignment was to show that we knew how to use the lab's new scanner and scanning software," I said, making up a story as I went along. "I took it one step further, for extra credit, to show that I'd learned our new graphics software, too. I was going to turn the assignment in to Mr. Saunders tomorrow when I have computer lab."

I looked at Mr. Saunders, hoping he would buy it.

"Well, Mr. Saunders, are you buying any of this?"

The computer teacher studied the letter, then studied me. I sat still.

"Actually, Mr. Rippleton," the teacher finally said, "this is the best piece of student work I've seen in a long time. It shows advanced computer skills along with critical thinking skills. Daniel will receive an A+ on this assignment."

The principal stared at my teacher for a long minute. Then he rolled his eyes back in his head.

"All right," Rippleton said. I could tell he was disappointed that he wouldn't be able to punish me again.

"You've slipped through my fingers this time, young man. But remember, you're on my most wanted list. I'm watching you. Everyone back to class." He stomped into his office and slammed the door.

"You owe me," Mr. Saunders said before he left the office. "I'll let you know just how you're going to pay that debt."

I breathed a huge sigh of relief and wiped my sweaty palms on the sides of my jeans. I followed Mr. Saunders out the door.

I didn't know how I was going to make it to the end of the week. It was only Tuesday.

Chapter 3
The Bully Brigade

I was surprised at just how smoothly the rest of the week went. To pay him back, Mr. Saunders kept me busy in the computer lab. I had to clean computer screens, polish scanner glass, and change ink cartridges every day.

I found out why I hadn't seen Willy, too. He got sick over the weekend and missed three days of school. He was back on Thursday but was still too weak to mess with anybody.

But now it was Friday. I got word from Jesse that Willy was feeling more like his old self. Isn't that nice for Willy, I thought. I turned my Willy radar back on and managed to steer clear of the bully all morning.

At noon I was rounding the corner on the way to the cafeteria when I ran straight into Willy and his "goon squad." My luck had just run out.

"Watch where you're going, Tonto," Willy said. He pushed me to the floor like I was a stack of straw. My books scattered everywhere. Willy and his friends laughed like fiends. I tried to ignore them and just began picking up my books and papers.

"What's the matter, redskin?" Willy taunted. "Leave your tomahawk back in the tipi?" Then he made Hollywood Indian war-whooping noises while his goons did the Atlanta Braves tomahawk chop. That did it.

I lunged into Willy, managing to land a hard right to his nose. We tumbled onto the floor. Willy's gang jumped on me. They landed several punches of their own.

Two nearby teachers broke up the fight almost as fast as it had started. But not before Willy and I each got a bloody nose and a black eye.

Of course, we were dragged into the principal's office yet another time. Mr. Rippleton was the judge and jury when it came to school rules. The school nurse cleaned up our bloodied faces while the principal paced back and forth in front of us. I dared not move a muscle.

"I'm calling both of your parents, you know," he said.

Willy and I spoke up at the same time. I blamed him. He blamed me.

"Frankly, I don't care who started the fight, gentlemen," the principal said. "I won't tolerate fighting in this school." He looked at Willy.

"I've come to expect this kind of brutish behavior from you, Mr. Phillips. It just seems to be part of your nature."

Then he walked over and stood looking down at me.

"But I'm disappointed in *you*, Mr. Wind. I thought those sessions we had with the counselor and your parents would have made a difference by now."

He began pacing again.

"I'm going to suspend both of you for three days. That'll give you and your parents plenty of time to consider the seriousness of the situation." He turned to the school secretary.

"Get their parents on the phone," he told her. "I want to give them this news personally!" He entered his office and closed the door behind him.

It was Bill who showed up to take me home. I knew there would be a lecture, followed by a serious grounding. What I got was much worse. Much worse.

"Your mother is very disappointed in you," Bill said in the car. "She told me she didn't want to see you or talk to you until tonight."

That was it. No yelling. No threatening. Just a message. This was serious. When we got home, I went straight to my room and just lay on my bed—for a long time.

When Mom got home she stayed busy in the kitchen. I could hear her in there clanging pans and rattling pots.

Bill brought me a tray of food at dinnertime. He left it on the desk without saying a word. But I couldn't eat. I just waited.

At around eight o'clock, I couldn't stand it anymore. I got up and went into the living room. Mom had changed out of her business clothes and put on a pair of old jeans and a denim shirt. Now she looked more like the mom I'd always known.

"Yell at me or ground me or something, Mom," I pleaded. "I can't take this silent treatment." I dropped down on the couch next to her.

I'm glad none of my friends were around, because she took me in her arms just like she used to do when I was little. I calmed down and looked into her eyes.

"Tell me the story, Mom." My voice seemed small and distant. "Tell me how you and Dad moved from the reservation to the city. I haven't heard it in a long time."

She smiled and reached over to the coffee table. Picking up our old family photo album, she opened it to the first page. I leaned against her shoulder. Inside the book was a faded picture of a young American Indian couple. She pointed to the picture.

"Your father and I were young when we got married. We were struggling to make a living out on the reservation," she began. "We lived with your grandma and grandpa in a small frame house."

She pointed to a picture of an older American Indian couple in front of a wood-frame house. She turned the page to a picture of my dad riding horseback.

"One day your father heard about a new government program that trained Indians how to do new jobs," she continued. "The only catch was that we had to move to a city to learn the skill and get a job." The next picture showed Mom and Dad standing in front of a pickup truck loaded with furniture and suitcases.

"We moved into a house that the Bureau of Indian Affairs found for us on the lower east side of Los Angeles. Your dad began training for his new job as a welder." The next picture showed my dad holding a welding torch and mask.

"Then, a few years later, you were born." A turn of the page took us to a picture of Mom and Dad holding a little brown baby with a bushy head of black hair.

"That's when we took a trip back home to Montana, to Rocky Point, to show you off to the family." She turned to a photo taken on the reservation with all of our family standing around. "Your uncle Robert and your grandparents were so proud."

That made Mom think of something.

"Your uncle Robert," she said, closing the photo album. "I haven't talked to him in a long time." She put the album back on the coffee table.

"Son, we're going to get through this," she said with a serious tone. "I know you still miss your father. I do, too. And even though I don't approve of fighting, I bet he would have been proud of you today."

I certainly didn't expect those words to come out of my mother's mouth.

"One of the teachers who broke up the fight told me what Willy did to make you go after him," she explained. "Your father had to put up with the same kind of insults when we first moved here. He got into fights over it, too."

"Sometimes it really sucks," I said. "Why did we have to be born Native American, anyway? We don't seem to fit in with other kinds of Americans."

"I know it seems like that sometimes," she sighed. "But, according to the Indian way of looking at things, each race of man has a special place in this world. A special gift or job set for us by the Creator. Our task, the Indian task, is to protect the earth and all the plants and animals that live on the earth with us. Our special gift is knowing that all things on this earth are related. This is what my grandmother taught me."

I had to think about that for a minute.

"It all sounds really nice, Mom, but not really relevant in today's world."

She took a deep breath. "Relevant? When did you start using such big words?" She stood up. "What's relevant is the fact that you've been suspended from school," she continued. "I have to find something to do with you for three days next week while I'm at work. So I want you to go to your room and listen to

Road Kill or Road Warriors or whatever their name is and let Bill and me talk about this."

Bill again. Why did *he* always have to be involved?

I marched into my room and closed the door. Cranking up Road Warriors, I put on my headphones. I dove into the food Bill had left for me earlier like I hadn't eaten for a week. "Don't Hate Me" rocked full blast in my head.

Chapter 4
Exiled

I stayed in my room while Mom and Bill talked about what to do. They didn't know that I could hear what they were saying through the air conditioning vent. She told him about my uncle Robert who lived on the reservation.

"Robert is a social worker for the Rocky Point Tribe," Mom told Bill. "He's an experienced horseman and all-round outdoorsman. I have a feeling that he might have some ideas about how to help Danny."

Bill agreed that Mom should call him, at least to see if he did have ideas.

When Saturday came, Mom said I was grounded and wouldn't be going to baseball practice. She and Bill had decided I would clean out the garage instead. While I was doing that, she called my dad's brother, Robert, on the Rocky Point Reservation. They talked about me.

Then, that afternoon, when Bill came home after working half a day at the bank, he and Mom talked about me some more.

By the time the garage was clean, I'd had enough. I couldn't stay on the sidelines while my future was being decided. I walked in on Mom and Bill in the middle of their talk.

"I want to know what's going on. I want to have a vote in what happens. I'm old enough now."

"All right," Mom said. "Sit down."

That was a surprise. I sat on the couch.

"Robert said this is an important time in your life," she said. "You are starting to make the change from boyhood to manhood. You need to go through a rite of passage to mark this change."

"What's a rite of passage? I've never heard of that."

"It's something you do to help you go from child to adult," Mom said. "Different tribes have different ways of doing that, Robert said. It's a kind of challenge you have to complete."

That sounded a little scary. "What kind of challenge?" I asked.

"We'll get to that. Your uncle holds a camp in the summer for American Indian teenagers for just that purpose. He invited you to come up this summer for the camp."

"You mean go to Montana?"

"That's right. You can stay with Robert and your cousins. Oh, and your grandma and grandpa live with them, too. You haven't seen any of them since you were little."

Spend a couple of weeks in the middle of nowhere? How could they even think I'd be okay with that?

"Sounds like a terrible idea," I said loudly.

"Robert wants you spend the summer with them so you can really find out about your tribal roots. He thinks it will also help you move on from the loss of your dad."

"The whole summer? That's the worst torture I could imagine! You really worked hard to come up with this punishment."

I paced back and forth just like Mr. Rippleton had.

"This isn't punishment," Bill said. "It's about having new experiences and learning to become a man. It will build character. It's . . ."

"Three months of tedious boredom." I finished the sentence. "They probably don't have phones, TV, or even electricity out there! I bet they don't even have indoor plumbing."

"Now you're being overly dramatic," Mom said. "Things have changed there. They're quite modern these days."

"You mean they finally discovered toilet paper?"

That wasn't the right thing to say, but I was mad. It made Mom mad, too.

"You can just take that attitude straight to your bedroom, young man." She pointed toward the hall. "And don't come out until I tell you to."

I marched to my room again and plopped down on the bed. Life isn't fair. I lay there, tossing and turning and feeling so angry. I decided to try my hand at my Star Fox computer game. As I shot down the enemy jet fighters, I imagined that each one was Mr. Rippleton or Willy Phillips or Bill. But I lost focus and went down in a fiery ball of flames.

Just then, there was a knock at my door. Bill stuck his head in.

"I'd like to talk to you for minute, if I could," he said.

Now what? I sighed and turned off the game. Bill came in and sat on the edge of the bed.

"I know it's been hard for you," he said. "You lost your dad and a stranger moved into your life."

"You got that right. It's not fair."

"I know, but I want you to think seriously about this summer as a chance to start over. It could be a wonderful time for you to explore your own roots and learn about a part of who you are."

"What would you know about it?" I asked, glaring at him. "You're not Indian."

"You don't have to be Native American to know the pain of losing someone you love. Or what it means to discover an unknown part of yourself."

"I guess *you* don't know about that."

"I'm from a Scottish family. But those roots were lost to me when my father abandoned my mother and went back to Scotland when I was a boy."

"That must have been tough," I said.

"It was. And it wasn't until after I grew up that I went to Scotland to find him and discovered my roots. It made all the difference to me. Things in my life made more sense."

Whoa. I never knew this about Bill.

"Besides, you can take your laptop computer and send e-mails back and forth to Jesse every day. There's bound to be some kind of Internet access there."

I realized that Mom and Bill and Uncle Robert had already made up their minds. I wasn't going to win this one.

"Okay, I'll go on one condition—that you let me come back home after the camp, if I hate it out there. Deal?"

"Deal," Bill said, and we shook hands.

Chapter 5
The Middle of Nowhere

My final weeks of school zipped by quietly. Mr. Saunders had me cleaning computer screens and maintaining the lab's printers for the rest of the year to pay off my debt to him.

Most important, I managed to stay out of trouble, and so did Willy. He even apologized to me on the last day of school for the "culturally insensitive remarks" he'd made. Miracles do happen, I guess. Somebody must've really threatened him with very severe punishment to get him to say that. Did he even know what the words meant?

Bill and Mom rewarded my good behavior at school with a trip to the mall to get me stuff for my summer adventure. They bought me some new clothes and my first cell phone, with a few game apps for the trip.

Washing clothes and packing came next. Mom spent one whole day getting things ready. But it was up to me to pack all the real necessities of life: my laptop computer and accessories (just in case they *did* have electricity and phones), games, comic books, junk food, etc.

Then, in the middle of June, it was time to head to Montana. Mom couldn't bear the thought of me flying alone and changing planes in an airport so far away. She decided the bus was the way for me to go.

She cried a little when I boarded. She said something about her baby leaving the nest. It was so embarrassing. As for me, I'd agreed to go along with the whole deal. But that didn't mean I was happy about it.

Bill had showed me on the map the route the bus would take. It headed north from Los Angeles on Interstate Highway 15 and passed through southern Nevada and Utah. During the first part of the ride, I kept busy as best I could. I watched the scenery out the window, slept, played games, and drew dragons on my computer.

In Salt Lake City, everyone got off the bus to eat dinner in a little roadside cafe. When we got back on the bus, an old man who smelled like drugstore shaving lotion sat down next to me. The smell was so strong I had to excuse myself and move to the back of the bus so I could breathe.

The sunset was amazing that day. Out there, away from the city, the sky seemed clearer. The big windows on the bus made everything seem closer, too. White puffy clouds moved across the sky. They changed colors, to orange and red, as the sun went down.

Moved by the wind, the clouds swirled around and made different shapes. For just a minute, they looked like a herd of buffalo stampeding across the sky. I'd never seen anything like it. But in the next minute, the animals melted into a row of cotton balls floating on a piece of dark blue cloth. Then the sun was gone.

After that, I was too bored to do anything else. I slept during most of the rest of the ride through Idaho and across Montana. I woke up the next morning as the bus pulled into the station at Billings, Montana.

I looked for the grandparents I kind of remembered from when I was little. I didn't see them. But I did see a very old man and woman who sort of looked like them.

It was easy to tell they were Indians. The man had dark brown wrinkled skin and long white hair tied in two long braids. The white-haired woman had lighter skin and a single braid like mine.

"Danny?" the man said.

"Grandpa, is that you?"

It was them. Mom reminded me that their names were Ester and Nathan Wind. That's where my middle name, Nathan, came from. The couple said they were very happy to see me.

I didn't see how they could have anything to do with me. As far as I could tell, we had nothing in common. But I was polite to them, just as I'd promised Mom I would be.

They helped me gather up my things. We loaded it all into their old station wagon. While Grandpa Nathan drove, Grandma Ester tried to carry on a conversation with me. I mostly just said "uh-huh" and "nuh-uh" to her questions about me and my life in L.A.

It took about us an hour to drive to the Rocky Point Indian Reservation. I still couldn't get over the wide open spaces and the clear blue sky. As we entered the reservation, we passed through a place called Buffalo Gap, the reservation's main town.

I watched everything we passed, because I needed to know where I could find junk food if I ran out. Or what store might have movies to rent. If I was going to be stranded in the middle of nowhere for the summer, it was important to know how bad the situation really was.

We passed the Rocky Point tribal office, a pizza parlor, a video store, a feed and hardware store, a gas station, and a few other shops. I was surprised by all these "modern" conveniences.

A few more miles of driving among the hills and fields took us to Robert's house. Grandpa called it the Wind family home. It looked really run-down to me.

There was a plain older house, a couple of horse corrals, a barn, and two sheds that kind of leaned to one side. A tractor and a pickup truck were parked out by the barn. A broken-down old Chevy was turning to rust beside the house.

"We all live here together," Grandpa said as we got out of the car. "Three generations sharing one house. Many families on the reservation live together, making the best of what they have." The look on my face must have told Grandpa I wasn't impressed. "Your father grew up in this house," he added.

That was good to know. A connection to Dad. "I'm sure it'll be fine," I said. "I'm just tired and hungry."

"Well, let's see what we can do about that," Grandpa said with a smile.

Inside I met my uncle's new wife, Amanda, and my cousins, Crow and Rabbit. Grandpa said we were all very small when we saw each other the last time. I didn't remember.

Amanda was a pretty American Indian woman. She welcomed me to their house and said it was always good when someone in the family came home for a visit.

"It might seem a little crowded at first," Amanda said. "But I'm sure you'll get used to it. You'll be outside most of the time anyway. Crow and Rabbit are."

Crow was thirteen and Rabbit was twelve. They didn't seem so friendly.

"My dad said you were getting into trouble at school," Rabbit announced. "That's why they sent you here, to straighten you out." Great. Everything out in the open. At least I knew where I stood with them.

"That'll be enough out of you, young man," Grandma said to Rabbit. She pushed the younger boy into the living room.

"Crow, why don't you help Danny get settled into your room?" Grandpa suggested.

Crow led me toward the back of the house to their room. It was a small room with two sets of bunk beds.

"You can take this bunk near the door," Crow said. "It's where company always sleeps when we have a ceremony or a powwow." I dumped my stuff on the lower bunk and looked around. There were three posters on the wall: a powwow dancer, some rock 'n' roll band, and a picture of a woman in a red bathing suit named Pamela Anderson from an old TV show.

Amanda brought in some clean sheets and bed covers for my bed.

"Crow, why don't you show Danny around the place while I fix his bed," she said. Then she told him something in the Cheyenne language, which I didn't understand. In English, she added, "Dinner will be ready in just a little while."

In my tour of the house, I found that they did have electricity, telephones, radio, and even TV. Rabbit was in the living room watching an old "Johnny Quest" cartoon, one of my favorites. Maybe this wasn't going to be so bad after all.

Crow led me outside to look around. I saw that the barn and corrals held horses, goats, and a few chickens. The natural surroundings were nice enough. But I was already getting homesick for the sounds of the city. Where were the cars, the jet planes, the sirens, the tall buildings, the McDonald's?

Crow went back inside the house, leaving me to explore a little on my own. I took a walk around the outside of the house. As I turned the corner to the side of the house, my eyes fell on a wonderful sight. It was a small gray satellite TV dish bolted to a cement pad in the ground. There was a black cable running from the dish into a socket on the side of the house. Digital satellite television! I was beyond excited.

I ran inside and found the TV remote control on the couch in the living room. The channel surfing began. All the great channels were there: MTV, Animal Planet, Nickelodeon,

Disney, Discovery Channel, Cartoon Network. I was in teen heaven.

It wasn't long before my uncle got home from work. I was watching an old episode of *Star Trek Voyager* when I heard him.

"Hi, Danny," he said loud enough to be heard over the TV.

"Uncle Robert!" I exclaimed, putting the TV on mute. I had forgotten what a big man he was. He had brown skin and was muscular like my dad. He even had the same single braid of long black hair down his back. He sat down next to me on the couch.

"It's good to see you, Danny. I'm glad you came."

"I'm sure I'll get used to it," I said hopefully.

"I know you haven't been out here in a long time. I also know that everything is different from what you're used to," Robert said. "Just relax and give it chance. Things are going to work out fine."

He smiled. I smiled back. It felt like a part of my dad was with me now.

"Let's go and see what your grandma and Aunt Amanda have fixed for dinner."

As we ate, Robert told the family about his plans for the summer. He had already signed up Crow, Rabbit, and me for part-time jobs with the tribe's summer youth program. Crow and Rabbit moaned at that news, but it sounded kind of cool to me. A summer job.

He said we'd be working as part of a "handyman" crew fixing up the homes of elderly tribal members a few hours a day. Our afternoons would be free, with time to help out with household and barnyard chores. Even I moaned when I heard *that* news.

"The wilderness survival camp will start the end of June," he said. "Crow and Rabbit will help me run the camp, like they've done for the last two summers." The two boys proudly puffed their chests out a little. I could tell they liked the camp. Being their father's assistants made it even better for them.

I, on the other hand, must have been frowning as Uncle explained the camp.

"Not much of a nature boy, Danny?" Crow teased. "Don't worry. Us wild country Indians will go easy on you, you being a civilized city Indian and all."

"Crow!" Robert said sternly. "Danny is family. And he's your guest, so act proper!" He finished the scolding in Cheyenne.

Crow ducked his head slightly. "Yes, Dad," he said.

After dinner, Crow and Rabbit were definitely more friendly.

I showed off my laptop computer to my cousins. They showed me where there was a phone jack to plug in and send e-mail from. I e-mailed my first report to Jesse back in L.A.

I also showed them a few of the graphics tricks I could do. Now it was my country cousins' turn to be impressed with this urban skin.

I went to bed with a jumble of thoughts going through my head. I had reconnected with Uncle Robert. And I had discovered that digital satellite TV had made it to the reservation. Now it seemed I'd be able to survive a summer here.

I was still worried about how I was going to fit in with the reservation routine, though. That was the last thought that went through my mind before I nodded off to sleep.

Chapter 6
The Buffalo People

Robert made sure we were up bright and early the next morning so we could get ready to report for our first day of work.

"Rise and shine, you sleepyheads," he blared. He was in way too good a mood for that time of morning. "Time to join the human race."

"Is he always this cheerful in the morning?" I asked my cousins sleepily.

"Yeah, Dad makes every day seem like a day at army boot camp," Crow replied, wiping the sleep from his eyes.

I could smell sausage and biscuits cooking in the kitchen. My brain cells began to kick into action. And so our summer routine began.

After breakfast, Robert took us to the tribal offices where he introduced me to the head of the summer jobs program.

Then we jumped into the back of a pickup truck filled with rakes, mowers, shovels, and hoes. We headed off to the first elder's home in need of repair.

Every morning we cleaned yards, mended fences, fixed walkways, painted walls, hauled off junk, and mowed lawns. The elderly residents were very grateful. They often gave us cookies, lemonade, and other goodies.

But I also had to work at being accepted by the other kids in the program. As a newcomer from the city, I took a lot of teasing.

Our afternoons were spent doing chores around the farm or ranch or whatever it was. With the help of Amanda, Grandpa, and my cousins, I learned how to care for the animals on the property.

In my spare time, I watched TV, worked on my computer, and exchanged emails with Jesse back home. I showed Crow and Rabbit how to access websites with images on the Internet. I also taught them how to take images from different sources, merge them together, and create new images. They thought it was pretty cool.

In exchange, Crow and Rabbit showed me how to ride horses. The family owned several of them. The horses were used to being ridden on a regular basis. So a couple of times a week, we headed out for the reservation's wide open spaces. There ain't nothin' in L.A. like that.

One afternoon, after I had finished my barnyard chores, Grandpa Nathan took me into the house. He led me to a back room where he kept his special collection of old American Indian stuff. He sat me down on a campstool and took a seat in a big, old, faded brown chair in the corner.

"Danny, what did your father teach you about the Cheyenne people before he died?"

"Not much that I can remember, Grandpa. He was always too busy working and trying to make a living for us. We did go to powwows sometimes. But I usually just played with other kids there."

"That's too bad," he said. He picked up a long wooden box with a black handle that sat on a table beside his chair.

"He always told me to be proud of being Cheyenne," I added. "He had a collection of old pictures of Cheyennes in the 1800s, like Black Kettle, that he used to show me."

"Did he tell you about the Pipe, or the Sun Dance, or the Buffalo People?" He placed the wooden box in his lap.

"No. What's the Buffalo People?"

"First things first," Grandpa answered. He opened the box and pulled back a piece of deerskin that covered what was inside.

"There are things that a Cheyenne boy of your age should start learning. Since your dad is gone, it will be up to your uncle and me to teach you these things."

"What kind of things?"

"Important things. Cheyenne things," Grandpa said.

He pulled an old metal TV tray from the other side of the chair and set it between us. Then he took four little plastic bags from the box and placed them on the tray. Grandpa opened the bags and poured what looked like cooking herbs out on the tray. What was all this stuff?

"I want to introduce you to four sacred gifts given to us by the Creator for our use," Grandpa continued. "These are sage, sweetgrass, cedar, and tobacco." He pointed at each as he spoke its name in Cheyenne. "Each one has a special use to help us as we perform our duties as human beings."

He reached once again into the box and took out a fan made of brown feathers. The handle of the fan was covered in beautiful beadwork. He put the fan nearby on the tray. Then he placed a metal bowl in the center of the tray.

He took a pinch of the cedar and dropped it in the bowl. Then he took a couple of sprigs of sage and crumbled them into the bowl. Reaching into his pocket, he pulled out a small lighter.

"Stand up," he said. I stood up.

"What are you going to do?" I asked.

"I'm going to give you a cleansing blessing," Grandpa replied. He fired up the lighter and put the flame into the bowl. That got the mixture of sage and cedar burning. A stream of smoke that smelled sweet came up from the bowl.

Taking the bowl in one hand and the feather fan in the other, Grandpa stood up. He began fanning the smoke toward me, spreading it over the front of my body. He sang a Cheyenne song as he fanned.

Suddenly I remembered my dad doing this ceremony for me on my first day of school. He had said I could do this for myself anytime I was bothered by something or before an important event. I had totally forgotten about it.

I stayed quiet and let Grandpa finish the ritual. Next, he stepped behind me. Grandpa fanned the smoke all over my back and legs and the top of my head.

"Okay, that's all for today," Grandpa said. He sat down in his big stuffed chair. "We'll start 'Indian school' tomorrow after your chores." He began putting the items back in the box.

I was a little puzzled about what had taken place. Just as I was about to ask a question, Grandpa said, "I'll explain a little at a time as we go along. Tomorrow, we'll start with the Buffalo People. Now run along and play with your cousins." He smiled.

And so it began. Almost every day after I finished my chores, I'd sit with Grandpa in the back room listening to tales of the days of Cheyenne glory. But Grandpa was really interested in telling me about the buffalo. He had books with paintings, drawings, and photographs of the animals.

"The Buffalo People were the Creator's greatest gift to our people," Grandpa said. "We got almost everything we needed for life from them. But we did not take life from our Buffalo Brothers for the sport of it. First we asked their permission, respectfully. Then we used everything that they had to offer. We wasted nothing. And we honored them with our songs and dances. We were spiritually connected to them."

"Spiritually connected? What does that mean?"

"It means they were part of us. And we were part of them. That's why we called them our brothers."

My grandfather's stories painted beautiful pictures in my mind of the olden days. That was a time when the Cheyenne people were free and lived close to the earth. Grandpa longed for those "good old days." Back then, the buffalo roamed the plains and the Cheyenne moved their camps regularly to be near them.

"When a herd of the great beasts started a stampede, they made a loud rumble you could hear for miles," he said. "It sounded just like thunder the plains. That was a thrill!"

My mind became filled with fantasies about those days. At night I dreamed about those powerful animals. Sometimes they could talk to me. And I could communicate with them. They told me they missed the old days too, when we played together. One night I dreamed that I was a Cheyenne hunter in the 1800s. I pictured myself riding on horseback across the plains with a hunting party in search of a herd. I woke up and my heart was pounding with excitement!

Chapter 7
In My Father's Footsteps

The time for survival camp finally arrived. We got our camping gear ready. On the last Saturday of June, Amanda cooked our final meal before we left. It was a hearty country breakfast of eggs, bacon, biscuits, and jelly.

Amanda and my grandparents stood in the front doorway of the house. They waved as we pulled out in Uncle Robert's pickup. We were headed to the tribal community center in Buffalo Gap.

On the way to the center, Robert said, "Danny, during camp I'm going to treat you like I treat everyone there. So don't expect any special favors. Got that?"

"Okay."

"It's for your own good. That way you'll get the most out of the week."

"Okay." That's all I could think to say.

We were the first ones to arrive at the tribal community center. We had to be there early so my uncle could greet the kids and their parents. A half dozen teenagers from other communities on the reservation were dropped off that morning.

According to my uncle, these were kids who had been in some kind of serious trouble. We all kind of sized each other up as we waited for everyone else to arrive. One of the boys reminded me of my "favorite" bully back home, Willy.

When all the campers had arrived, Robert called us together.

"Okay kids, listen up," Robert commanded. "You're mine for a week. Mommy and Daddy won't be here for you to run to or to kiss your boo-boos. I'm your mother, father, and teacher." Everyone laughed nervously when he said the word "mother."

"And if you get out of line," he continued, "I'll be judge, jury, and executioner." We stopped laughing. All of a sudden I had scary visions of Mr. Rippleton.

"During your stay with me, you will learn to work together, like it or not," he declared. "You'll obey my orders at all times. We'll be heading into some rough country, facing unpredictable weather situations. Your life could depend on doing exactly what I say, when I say it. Got that?"

Nobody said a word.

"Got that?" he repeated loudly.

"Yes, sir," a few of the teens replied weakly.

Robert walked over to the biggest kid in the group. The guy was leaning against the side of the building. My uncle grabbed him by the collar of his shirt and pulled him upright.

"I can't hear you!" Robert yelled right in this kid's face. He sounded like a boot camp sergeant.

"YES, SIR!" the kid barked. Every kid in the group was paying attention now.

My uncle smiled. "Now that's more like it," he said. "What's your name, young man?" he asked softly.

"Cutnose, sir. Ben Cutnose," he answered. Now he sounded nervous.

Robert let go of the kid's collar and straightened it out neatly.

"All right, Ben. Now that we've got that straight, let's begin. Pick up your gear and follow me." He led all of us around to the back of the community center. Crow and Rabbit had ten horses waiting for us, saddled and ready to go. Robert easily mounted his.

"Okay, mount up," he said. Nobody moved.

"What are you waiting for?"

Crow and Rabbit jumped up on their steeds. I was up on my horse next. My summer riding lessons were paying off. The rest of the kids struggled to get up on their animals. Some were having more trouble than others.

"Worse than I thought," Robert said. "Have any of you ridden before?" One girl raised her hand.

"Oh, this is sad," Robert said, shaking his head. "Your Cheyenne ancestors are turning over in their graves."

He got off his horse.

"All right, we'll start at the beginning." He walked over to the girl who had raised her hand.

"What's your name, young lady?"

"Charlene," she said.

"Charlene, can you demonstrate the right way to mount a horse?"

"I believe so."

"Go right ahead then," Robert said.

She got off her horse, then got back on again. She smoothly put one foot in the stirrup and swung the other leg over the horse's back. She made it look easy.

"Very good," Robert said. "Now everyone else try it." He got back on his horse. All of us finally got mounted.

"Okay, let's head out," he said. He backed his horse away from them. "I'll go easy on you this first day to let you get used to being on horseback. Don't let the horse know that you're scared. He'll sense it. If that happens, you won't be able to control him."

He led us away from the tribal offices and out onto the flat grassy plain. As we rode along, he took time to explain certain riding techniques. He showed us how to sit in the saddle the right way. How to lead the horse in the direction you want him to go. How to trot and gallop.

Our first day on the trail was pretty easy. We all had fun learning to ride and taking in the beautiful scenery.

I'm not certain, but during that first day, it seemed like Charlene kept moving her horse near mine on the trail. Maybe I just imagined it.

Around sunset, we rode into a campsite that was made of a circle of tipis around a center fireplace. As I got off my horse, I realized for the first time just how sore my bottom was. I looked around and saw that everyone seemed to be having the same feeling. The moaning and groaning was pretty loud.

After eating a simple dinner, we chilled around the campfire. The kids were tired from the day's ride and feeling a little sleepy. Robert got us talking about ourselves, where we were from and what we liked and didn't like. Ben Cutnose decided to start picking on me.

"One of the things I really don't like is these urban skins who come out here and try to pretend they're real Indians," he said while glaring at me.

"I'm not pretending to be anybody or anything," I told him.

"Yeah? Well, why don't you pack up and run home to mama before you get hurt!"

"I'm not afraid of you or anybody else," I said, just before I grabbed him and pushed him to the ground. We rolled around in the grass. I tried to get control of him. He tried to get control of me. Then a couple of other kids jumped in on top. Finally, Crow and Rabbit piled on to help me.

While everyone was focused on the fight, Robert pulled a pistol out of his backpack and fired it into the air twice. Everyone froze in place. Ben and I did the same.

"Get up!" Robert ordered. "All of you. Back to your seats . . . NOW!" I had never seen kids move so fast. We all scurried back to our places.

"You just earned yourselves an early bedtime tonight and extra camp chores tomorrow," Robert said. "You've got a tough week ahead of you. It's going to take teamwork to make it through. So you'd better leave the attitude here in this place tonight."

Quietly, we all shuffled off to our tipis.

Curled up in my bedroll, I tossed and turned. I couldn't to go to sleep. After awhile, I got up and went back out to sit near what was left of the campfire. Robert was already there. He was making notes in a notebook by flashlight. I sat down on a log and began poking the coals with a stick.

"Want to talk about it?" Robert asked, looking up from his notebook. "I know something's eating at you. This trip is the time to get it out."

I poked at the coals for a bit more. Robert waited.

"I don't fit in anywhere," I finally said. "The kids at home tease me because I'm Indian.

They tease me out here because I'm not Indian enough. If only my dad hadn't died."

"I know," Robert said. "I miss him too. As far as big brothers go, he was the best. And he went through some of the same things you're going through. It's hard to be Native anywhere. It wasn't any easier for your dad when he had to move to L.A. to learn a trade, get a job, and support his family."

He closed the notebook and moved closer to me.

"Your dad had a hard time fitting in. He missed this reservation terribly. It was the only life he knew. But he swallowed his pride and did his duty. I was proud of him for it. And I know you can do this, too. You've got his blood. You'll figure out how to either find a place or make a place for yourself. And I know that one day you'll make your father proud of you, too."

"Thanks, Uncle Robert," I said. "You sounded just like my dad there for a minute."

"I'll take that as a compliment. Now let's hit the sack. We've got a long day ahead of us." We walked toward the tipi together.

"You know you really scared us when you fired that gun," I told him. "Aren't you worried that somebody might accidentally get hurt with it?"

"Not really," Robert chuckled. "It's only loaded with blanks. I just carry it to scare off animals. They run from it almost as fast as you guys did."

Boy, was I relieved! I laughed as I stepped into my tipi. I settled into my bedroll and fell fast asleep.

Chapter 8
You Can Blame John Wayne

The next morning, Robert headed the horses toward rougher terrain. The flat grassy meadows faded away behind us. Ahead were jagged hills and ridges.

It turned out to be a busy day. We learned how to mark trails, find directions, locate wild plants we could eat, and other interesting stuff. Robert let Crow and Rabbit show us some of the things they had learned last year on the trail.

Now things were starting to get cool. At the end of the day we were all in a good mood. We set up our tents for sleeping and joked with each other around the campfire that night.

"There's one thing you guys have out here on the rez that really beats the city," I said, looking up at the night sky.

"What's that?" Robert asked.

"An awesome view of the stars."

They all looked up.

"My grandma told me that we Cheyenne came from the stars," Charlene said. "And when we die, our spirits go back there."

"The Star People," Robert said. "It's good that you know this legend," he said to Charlene. "Do you know the rest of the story?"

"No, that's all I remember," the girl replied. "My grandma passed away last year. I wish I had listened to her more." She looked at me with eyes that said she knew I had lost my dad.

"The elders say that the Cheyenne people once lived up among the stars," Robert explained. "They looked down upon the earth and thought it would be a good place to live. One night a long, long time ago, the Creator caused a great shower of stars to fall to Earth. Those stars were the Cheyenne People. The Creator had given us this part of the world to live on."

No one spoke for a few minutes. We all thought about the story and gazed at the sky.

That made me think of a question.

"Uncle Robert, why do some white people give Indians a hard time? Sometimes it seems like they just hate having us around."

"It's kind of complicated, Danny," Robert said. Some of them still believe in something called Manifest Destiny. This is an idea from the 1800s. It's based on the belief that God gave them this America as their promised land."

"My dad said it was John Wayne's fault," Ben said. "A lot of white people grew up watching his Westerns. Those movies taught them that we were savages and worshipped the devil."

"That's part of it, too," Robert replied. "Other, more educated, people feel guilty about how Indians were treated, but they don't know what to do about it. So they don't like to think about it. That's just the way people are. But we know the truth, don't we."

He looked up at the sky. "We are descendants of the Star People."

Everyone was silent again for a while.

This time Robert broke the silence. "Okay, we've got a hard day tomorrow. Off to bed with you."

Robert ignored our protests. We headed for our tents. I felt a new sense of pride about being a Cheyenne Indian. I think the other kids did too.

On our third day we left the horses in a corral along the trail. We made sure the animals had plenty of food and water. Then we hiked away on foot. The going was much harder. We grew too tired to act cool or tease each other. By the end of the day, we were really dragging.

In camp that night there was little talk. No one had the energy. After dinner, each person quietly took care of his or her camp chores. I checked my tent to make sure that all the ropes were tight and my stuff was safely stowed inside.

I heard approaching footsteps. I looked up to see Charlene headed my way. She handed me a candy bar as I stood up.

"From my secret stash," she said as she unwrapped her own.

"Thanks," I said as I unwrapped mine.

"You ride pretty good for someone who's lived in the city all his life," she said.

"My cousins have been teaching me the past few weeks," I said between bites. "You have horses at home?"

"Yeah, my family is involved in Indian rodeo. I've picked up a few pointers."

We chewed our candy in silence for a few moments. Then Robert yelled that it was time for "lights out."

"Thanks for the candy bar," I told her. "It was good."

"Good night, Danny," Charlene said sweetly. "Sleep tight. See you in the morning."

I watched her as she walked to her tent. She was a nice girl. My uncle walked up to me a moment later and smiled. He nudged me in the arm and said, "Cute, huh?"

I blushed and quickly ducked inside my tent. Everyone else crawled into their tents. They probably passed out as fast as I did.

The group awoke the next morning to a blanket of grey clouds. It was the fourth day of our journey. Later in the day, a thunderstorm moved in as we hiked up a low hill. As the rain started, we stopped at the mouth of a shallow cave. We pulled out our ponchos and put them on.

We were at the base of a mountain. Robert pointed to a small path on the side of the mountain that zigzagged toward the top. It looked dangerous.

"That's where we're headed today," he said. "You're going to need teamwork to get up that path. Focus on what you're doing. Take each step carefully."

He showed us how to form a human chain using ropes. That way we were connected. If anyone slipped, the people on either side of them could help.

Then he arranged us in a line, boy-girl, boy-girl. My uncle took the lead and placed Crow at the end of the line. I was in the middle of the line with Charlene in front of me and another girl, Natalie, behind me.

Charlene gave me a nervous smile as we started walking. The rain wasn't heavy, but it was steady. It made the rocks slippery. Each foot had to be placed right in front of the other. No one spoke. No one joked.

We slowly worked our way up the trail. We went on for almost three hours without any problems. Finally, we came to another shallow cave in the side of the mountain. Robert signaled it was time for a break. We were glad to have a place to get out of the rain for a while.

"You're doing very well," Robert told us. "We'll rest here for a few minutes. But we can't stay too long or the sun will go down before we reach the top. We don't want to be on this trail after dark."

I understood why. The trail sure seemed tricky in more than a few spots.

After a brief rest, Robert said we had to go. The rain was still coming down. By around three o'clock we were all very tired and wet. The nonstop patter of the rain made me sleepy. I think everyone was having a hard time staying alert.

I tried to stay focused on my feet and the ground in front of me. I forgot that I was roped to one girl in front and another in back in a chain.

Then I noticed that the path turned past a big rock ahead and got very narrow. I couldn't see around the rock.

Suddenly, there was a scream from Charlene's direction and a hard pull on the rope. At once, I was jolted out of my daze. I leaned in toward the mountain as I pulled on the rope. I moved around the rock and saw Charlene dangling from the edge of the path. She was crying and screaming and trying to grab on to the side of the cliff. I was frozen for a moment. What was I supposed to do?

I looked ahead and saw that the next boy in front of her, James, had found something to hold on to while pulling on Charlene's rope. Suddenly I knew what to do.

"Hold on tight!" I yelled to James. "I'm going to try to pull her up." He nodded and tightened his grip. I knelt down on the gravel path and began to pull Charlene up hand over hand by the rope.

Meanwhile, Robert worked his way down the rope chain just in time to help me pull Charlene back up onto the path. She was shivering, cold, and scared. She hugged me. I hugged her back. That was a close one.

"Are you all right?" Robert asked. Charlene was too shaken to speak. She nodded her head and stepped back from me. She looked down at her legs. One knee of her jeans was torn. There was blood on it.

"We're almost to the top," Robert said. "Come up to the front with me. We'll finish the path together."

He disconnected her section of rope from me and attached her hook to his.

"Good work, Danny," he said, and gave me a pat on the back. Charlene said thank you with her eyes as Robert escorted her away.

In another hour, we made it to the top, just as the rain stopped. It was getting dark, so we quickly set up camp in a clearing at the top of the mountain.

We were soaking wet and shaken by what had happened. It was like we were taking life seriously for the first time, because danger and death had seemed so close.

That night, dinner was made up of protein bars, dried fruit, and water. We were glad to have that stuff as we warmed ourselves around a small fire. Robert bandaged Charlene's injured leg with supplies from the first aid kit.

After dinner, I left the circle and went to my tent. I rummaged around in the bottom of my backpack until I found what I was looking for. I went back and sat down beside Charlene and slipped her a candy bar.

"You're not the only one with a secret stash," I said with a smile. We laughed as we enjoyed our little treat.

The next morning I woke up and stepped outside my tent. Spreading out in front of me was most awesome view I had ever seen. The sky was clear. I could see for miles. Hills, valleys, mountains, trees, and meadows were all spread out before me. Now I know why people call the state "Big Sky Country."

After breakfast, Uncle Robert performed the same blessing ceremony for us that Grandpa had performed for me. With my help, Robert bathed the kids in the smoke with the sweet smell. He explained the meaning of the ceremony. And he told us about the four gifts that Grandpa had told me about: sage, sweetgrass, cedar, and tobacco. Some of the kids had never heard of these things. Their families had stopped doing traditional activities.

He told us we could perform this ceremony whenever we needed to cleanse ourselves, our minds, or our homes. Then he held up a sprig of prairie sage.

"Sage is a special gift used in the sweat lodge and during the Sun Dance. Its smoke doesn't burn your eyes or bother your nose."

He put the sage back down. "Now I have a special treat for you," Robert said. "Follow me."

He led us over a little rise to an open area. There was a beautiful field of wild sage.

"This is a secret field of sage, known only to a very few members of our tribe. It's where the great medicine men and warriors of our nation have picked their sage for generations." We walked into the field.

"Now it's your turn, as modern spiritual warriors, to pick your own sage to use when you need it."

We spent the morning picking the plants and relaxing in the field. Charlene stayed close to me as we picked our sage. We helped each other tie the long stems together into bundles.

Robert said we had finished the hardest part of our survival experience. He said that picking the sage was our reward. It was time to head back down the mountain.

On the way down, Robert pointed out Yellowstone National Park. I looked where he was pointing and could see it in the distance. I knew that nothing in L.A. could match this view or give me this feeling.

The rest of the week was downhill all the way. We hiked back to our horses. Then we rode back toward our starting point.

On Saturday, we rode back into Buffalo Gap. Robert said he really felt good about the week's camp. He had been successful in getting another group of Indian kids to see life from a different point of view. And to think about the natural world more. He said the kids in the group had formed a bond that only comes when people face hard times together.

We all said good-bye to Robert and to each other. Then we headed off to return to our normal lives.

Before she left, Charlene gave me her phone number. It was written on the outside of an envelope. Her eyes got misty as she told me good-bye and ran to her parent's car.

I opened the envelope and took out a yellow sheet of paper with a note on it. The note said, "You are a special friend, Danny. I'll always remember you. Hope I can see you again this summer before you go back home. Love, Charlene."

I had never had a girlfriend before, but this sounded like a note from one. I didn't know what to think about it. And I didn't know what I was supposed to do. I put the note in my back pocket.

As I rode back to my uncle's house, I began thinking about how good one of Aunt Amanda's meals would taste and how I missed her cooking. That was much safer than thinking about Charlene.

Chapter 9
Our Brothers Need Us

The next day I got a phone call from L.A. It was my stepdad.

"Well, survival camp is over," Bill said. "I promised that you could come home now if things weren't going well."

"Are you kidding?" I said. "I'm having a great time here. There's nothing like it there in L.A."

"I'm glad to hear it, Danny. Your mother and I are very pleased with the reports we've been getting back from Robert on your improved attitude. Keep up the good work. We'll see you at the end of the summer."

"Bill?"

"Yes, Danny, what is it?"

"Thanks for making me take this trip," I said.

"You're welcome. I know things are going to be better now, for all of us."

I hung up the phone. I felt that I had taken the first step toward connecting with my stepdad.

The next day my cousins and I went back to our summer routine. We fixed elders' houses in the morning and did chores at home in the afternoon. We squeezed in a little TV watching and computer time in between.

One day blurred into another. Summer days do that. I began taking a daily horseback ride. I liked it a lot. It was better than riding a bike back home. And I got to practice helping Robert, Crow, and Rabbit round up their little herd of cattle. I was becoming a real Indian cowboy.

One night, we watched TV with Grandpa. A TV news report came on that made us all pay attention.

The reporter said that last winter several hundred buffalo from Yellowstone National Park had been slaughtered when they roamed outside the borders of the park. Nearby ranchers were afraid the animals might be carriers of a disease called brucellosis. This illness could infect their cattle herds and make them sick. The news report showed images of the buffalo being killed. Their bodies were loaded onto tractors and hauled away.

"Robert! Amanda! Come in here quick!" Grandpa yelled toward the kitchen. "You've got to see this."

Uncle Robert and Aunt Amanda came into the living room.

Yellowstone Park's head ranger came on camera. His name was Jasper Perkins. "It was too bad that so many of these fine animals had to be put to death," he said. "The ranchers of Montana complained to the governor about the bison. And the governor complained to the park service. There was nothing I could do."

"Bison?" I asked as I watched.

"That's another name for buffalo," my uncle said.

The TV newsman asked Mr. Perkins another question. "Were the bison tested to see if they actually did have brucellosis before they were slaughtered?"

"The state laboratory did a random test of a small number of animals," Perkins replied.

"And what did they find?"

"One of the five bison had the disease."

"And on the basis of that one small test the government killed more than one thousand untested animals?" The reporter was astonished.

"I'm afraid so," Perkins replied. You could see the park ranger didn't like it. "What's worse is that more animals will probably be put to death this coming winter unless someone does something about it."

Then an American Indian man named Martin Two Bulls was shown. He spoke for an organization called the Inter-tribal Bison Cooperative. Several Indian tribes with their own buffalo herds belonged to this group.

"The buffalo of Yellowstone that roam free are a symbol of American Indian culture, history, and economy," he said. "We must stop this slaughter from happening again. I ask for the help of people who are watching this news program. Please don't let them murder our brothers, the Buffalo People, again. The army did this in the 1800s to destroy our food supply and our way of life. Please don't let it happen again."

The news report ended on a close shot of Mr. Two Bulls. He had a single tear rolling down his cheek.

Grandpa was shocked. "We've got to do something," he said to Robert.

"What can we do?" Robert asked.

"Maybe the tribal council can do something," Grandpa suggested.

"Maybe," Robert replied.

"You know those guys," Amanda said. "They won't stick their necks out for something like this." She went back to the kitchen.

"It can't hurt to try," Robert said. "I'll see if the tribal council will listen to us at their next meeting."

The next day Robert called the tribal office and got us a slot on the council agenda. Their next meeting would be in two days.

Our whole family went to the tribal council chambers that day. There were eight men on the council. They were elected by the members of the tribe every four years. The council made decisions about tribal business.

Grandpa told me that tribal councils were created in 1934 by something called the Indian Reorganization Act. This way the U.S. government has a group within each tribe to do business with.

When it came their turn, Grandpa and Robert stood in front of the council. They told the council about the news report. Robert said they could use the tribe's cattle trucks to go to Yellowstone and pick up fifty bison to start the tribe's own herd.

"Many other tribes have begun their own herds," Robert said.

My uncle and grandfather made a good presentation. I was sure that once the council heard the story they would take some action. Instead, the council members made a lot of excuses for why they couldn't do anything right now.

"Just the other day, Barney, our tribal cattle manager, was telling me that the fences need mending" the tribal chairman said. "Our cattle transport truck is still broke down, too."

"I thought we voted to have that fixed," another council member replied.

"Yeah, but we never set aside the money to make the repairs," the council treasurer reminded them.

"Well, let's check the minutes," the tribal chairman suggested.

"We could, but I left them at home," the council secretary said. "I can go home and get them if you want to wait."

The council voted not to make a decision until more information could be gathered. I couldn't believe it. My own people wouldn't take action on such an important matter!

"Amanda was right," Robert said. "They are afraid to stick their necks out."

"They're a bunch of —" Grandpa started to say, but my uncle stopped him.

"We all know what you think of the council," Robert said. "No need to repeat it."

Robert wanted to stay for the rest of the meeting. There was another topic the council was discussing that Robert was interested in. I decided to take a look around the tribal offices.

Most of the offices were closed, but I noticed one open door. The sign on it said "Tribal Chairman, Buddy Spotted Horse." My curiosity got the better of me. I went in to take a look around.

The tribal chairman had a nice big office with a lot of stuff hanging on the walls: Indian paintings, awards, plaques, and certificates. Who knows what they were for. On his desk were many stacks of papers. I moved in closer to get a better look.

I noticed a stack of papers with the tribe's official seal stamped at the top. I picked up the top sheet from the stack and looked at it more closely.

It was the chairman's official stationery. Next to the stack were some letters that the chairman had signed.

Then I got an idea! In my mind, I flashed back to school in L.A. I remembered the little prank I pulled with the principal's stationery. I thought this time I could do something important.

Quickly, I glanced toward the door to make sure it was safe. No one was around. I took five or six sheets of the stationary from the stack. I grabbed one of the signed letters and quietly slipped out of the room.

I stepped back into the council room just as the meeting was ending. After the meeting, I showed the papers to Crow.

"What are you going to do with those?" Crow asked.

"Give Yellowstone National Park a reason to release fifty buffalo to us," I answered.

Crow's puzzled look told me he didn't understand what I was saying.

"Never mind now," I said. "I'll tell you later. Right now, I need you to do something for me. Can you find that list of phone numbers of the kids from survival camp?"

"I guess so," Crow said. "My dad has that somewhere at the house."

"Tomorrow, get on the phone and call them all to a meeting for next Saturday afternoon."

"What for?" Crow asked.

"We're going to rescue us some buffalo." I could hardly believe what I was saying. "But don't tell anyone else. It's our little secret for now."

I was able to sneak the papers home without Robert or Grandpa seeing them. The next day I began my buffalo rescue project. Using my computer and a scanner that was small enough to hold in my hand, I started creating a letter. The tribal chairman didn't know it, but he was about to write to park ranger Jasper Perkins at Yellowstone National Park. The letter asked the park to release fifty head of buffalo to Danny Wind and his "associates" on behalf of the Rocky Point Tribe.

On Saturday, Ben, Charlene, and a couple of the other kids made it to the meeting site: the Pizza Hut in Buffalo Gap. I revealed my plan to them.

"We're going to ride horseback for two days across the country to rescue a herd of buffalo and bring them back here to Buffalo Gap." Everyone looked shocked.

"You're nuts," Ben said. "What makes you think we can pull off a stunt like that?"

"A week in the wilderness with you guys," I said.

Charlene looked straight into my eyes. "If Danny thinks we can do it, then I say let's go for it."

I blushed. But it felt good to have her support.

After a few more minutes of discussion, the kids agreed to help out. This would be great. I was on a roll.

The next step in my plan called for a real leap of faith. I needed to ask Grandpa to take the forged letter to Jasper Perkins in person. This would make our story more believable.

I took the risk and laid the whole plan out for Grandpa. It was like lighting a match to a pile of gun powder. When I was finished, Grandpa whooped and hollered until I thought the whole house was going to come crashing in. He hugged me close and said, "When do we start?"

The next day, Grandpa took the letter to the park ranger. Mr. Perkins was pleased that someone wanted to do something for these animals. He said yes to the request.

Meanwhile, I began planning our rescue route. To do this, I used my laptop to access something online called the "geographic information system." I was able to find 3-D maps of the land we would have to cross. I plotted a route over the hills and through the area from Rocky Point Reservation to where the buffalo were kept in Yellowstone. That was about two hundred miles. Any way I looked at it, I realized this wasn't going to be easy.

Chapter 10
The Race Begins

In the early dark hours of the next Saturday morning, our rescue team gathered. Ben, Charlene, and two other kids showed up. Each had brought a backpack filled with food and clothing for the trip. My cousins and I brought enough horses for everyone.

Then Grandpa showed up. He had more supplies and a horse of his own. In his hand was a sack.

"What are you doing here, Grandpa?"

"You can't just herd buffalo around like you can herd cattle," Grandpa explained. "They're much too independent and willful. I know the prayers and songs to offer to the spirits of the Buffalo People to get them to cooperate. You need me."

I looked to the other kids. They all nodded.

"I guess you're in," I said. "What's in the sack?"

"War paint," Grandpa smiled. "You can't go on a dangerous mission like this without the proper preparation. Our ancestors painted themselves and their horses to bring courage, strength, and hope at times like these."

He opened the sack and spread out his paints. Then he marked each of our faces with a different design. He sang a Cheyenne prayer song for our protection.

Finally, he painted his own face. I saw pride fill my grandfather's eyes. When he was finished, Grandpa nodded that he was ready.

We mounted our steeds and headed across the country. We had food and supplies to last several days.

Uncle Robert and Aunt Amanda probably panicked when they found out we were gone. But Grandpa left a letter explaining what we were doing. The letter said everything would be all right.

"This is a journey into their own adulthood," Grandpa wrote in the letter. "This is what tribal youth did in the old days. Please don't let anyone try to stop us. These kids want to do this. I need to do this."

"This is foolishness," Robert said when he found the letter. "One old man and a bunch of kids out there alone. Someone could get seriously hurt or even killed." He crumpled the letter and threw it on the floor. Amanda hugged him and tried to calm him down.

"I think you're overreacting," she said. "We should talk about this."

He broke away from her hug.

"It's not that simple," he explained. "There are other factors to think about here."

She reached out and brought him back to her.

"Have a little faith," she urged. "You're the one who's always talking about staying in touch with our Indian roots and Mother Earth. Well, they believed you. Now they're willing to put those words into action. And you have to support them in this. Otherwise, your words mean nothing."

He thought about what she said and calmed down.

"All right," he said finally. "We'll try it your way. But I need to let the other kids' parents know what's going on."

He picked up the phone to call the first set of parents.

Meanwhile, out on the trail, it was a hard trip. We had to use everything we had learned at survival camp. We made it to Yellowstone in two days as planned. We were guided by my maps and Grandpa's stories.

On Sunday night, we made camp on a ridge overlooking the park headquarters. That night Grandpa told us a story he'd been saving. His story went like this:

When the Creator made the earth and all its creatures, two-leggeds and four-leggeds lived together in peace. That means the people and the animals. After many seasons, the Buffalo People began to think they were the most powerful beings in the world.

They also came to believe that this gave them the right to kill and eat all the others. But the people said, "This isn't fair. We humans and you buffalo were created equal. But if someone is going to be the most powerful, it should be us!"

The buffalo said, "We must settle this argument. Let's have a race to see who eats who." But the people didn't like this idea. A race would be unfair because the buffalo can run much faster than people. "Let the birds race in our place," said the people. "That would make it fair.'"

The buffalo agreed. The buffalo chose their fastest runner. The people picked four birds for the race— Hummingbird, Hawk, Meadowlark, and Magpie.

They chose a place called Buffalo Gap as the starting and ending point of the race. It had a hill in the distance as the halfway mark for turning around. Then a signal was given. The race began.

Buffalo took off in a flash! For a little while, Hummingbird kept up with him but soon fell back exhausted. So Meadowlark took over. But Buffalo kept far in the lead. At the halfway mark, Meadowlark fell behind and Hawk came on strong.

Suddenly Hawk got a burst of speed and flew out ahead of Buffalo. The people cheered. But he didn't last long at the front. Hawk's sudden burst of energy failed. He fell back as Buffalo took the lead once again.

It seemed that Buffalo could run forever. Then, from way in the rear, came a little dot of black and white. It was Magpie! She was slow but strong of heart.

As they neared the finish line at Buffalo Gap, Magpie steadily gained on the mighty Buffalo. But Buffalo was finally getting tired. She gathered all her strength for one last push. The humans and the buffalo were cheering at the finish line, calling out and jumping up and down.

At the last possible moment, Magpie shot ahead of Buffalo and won the race! The people went wild with happiness.

So the buffalo lost. The humans won. Ever since then, people have been considered more powerful than the buffalo and the other animals. And people have hunted the buffalo for food. But the Cheyenne remember what the magpie did. They never hunt or eat that special bird. And we never forget that the buffalo are our brothers. Their spirits strengthen us. And we treat them with respect, too.

Chapter 11
A Magical Journey

On Monday morning, we presented ourselves to ranger Jasper Perkins and the park officials. We told them we were ready to pick up their buffalo.

To our surprise, Robert and the tribal chairman were waiting for us in the ranger's office. Uh-oh. We all feared this meant the end of our plan. All that planning and riding for nothing. I thought we might spend the rest of the summer locked in leg irons working on a chain gang.

Grandpa went into the office and spoke to the men alone. In a few minutes, the four men came out of the office. The tribal chairman spoke first.

"Danny, I was extremely upset when I found out that you had forged my name on official tribal stationery to make this happen.

That's a very serious crime, as far as I'm concerned." He paused.

"But your grandfather told me that what you and the rest of the kids were doing was for the good of the tribe. He said the tribal council should be ashamed for not taking any action to protect these animals. He's right. They represent part of our history and culture."

He looked at Robert. "And your uncle, who I respect very much, agreed. These were harsh words, but sadly true," the chairman continued. "So I've asked Mr. Perkins here to release the buffalo to you. He has agreed. Bring 'em home with my blessings." The chairman smiled.

I was so relieved! I shook the chairman's hand and hugged my uncle. The rest of the gang jumped for joy and hooted and hollered. Then Mr. Perkins stepped over to me.

"Danny," he said, "because of your efforts, I've contacted Martin Two Bulls of the Inter-tribal Bison Cooperative. We're going to start a tribal bison program that will allow other tribes in the area to take some of our excess animals to build up their own bison herds."

That was great! Perkins shook my hand. "Good luck on your ride home, son," he said.

We, the Cheyenne buffalo rescuers, mounted our horses and rode to the buffalo stockade. There were fifty of the most wonderful creatures I had ever seen. Up close I could see they were large and powerful. Almost scary. A couple of them were pawing the ground and snorting loudly. One was banging his horns against the stockade fence.

What had I gotten us into?

Then Grandpa began singing his Buffalo Song. The beasts started to calm down. The stockade gate was opened. The buffalo moved out of the pen, following Grandpa as he sang. It was amazing! We moved in behind and around the small herd. We began the long trip back to the reservation.

It was a slow but magical journey. With Grandpa singing in the lead, the herd followed him as readily as a herd of old dairy cows heading to the barn.

On the second day of the trip, Grandpa guided his horse close to mine.

"The oldest member of the herd asked me to thank you for this," Grandpa said.

"What?" I asked. "What did you say?"

"These buffalo are grateful to be going home to be with their Cheyenne brothers," he continued.

"How do you know this?"

"I speak Buffalo," Grandpa replied. "My grandpa taught me. One day I'll teach you." He smiled and moved back over in front of the herd.

The trip back took longer than we expected. The bison were walking very slowly. Finally, we made it back to Buffalo Gap about noon on Wednesday. There was wild excitement when the people saw us coming toward the edge of town.

The Cheyenne people of Rocky Point recognized the importance of this day. They stopped what they were doing and stood in doorways and on porches to watch the sight. They were in awe as the beautiful beasts trotted majestically down their main street and into the tribe's cattle pasture. Tears came to the eyes of many elders as they welcomed their four-legged brothers to their home.

That evening, the tribal chairman held a huge feast to honor me and the other kids. Before dinner, I stood with the chairman in front of the guests.

"Tonight we're here to honor a young man who has shown courage, vision, and leadership," Chairman Spotted Horse said. "I'm just glad he's not old enough to run for tribal chairman. Otherwise, I might have a real fight on my hands come the next election," he laughed.

The chairman gave me a carved wooden buffalo as a gift from his office and the tribal council. Then he launched into a campaign speech for his re-election.

After dinner, Robert, Grandpa, and I stood together outside in the front of the house, talking and watching the sunset.

"I'm proud of both of you," Robert said. "You've reminded a lot of our people what can be accomplished when you believe in something strongly enough."

Grandpa smiled.

"But it was still a foolhardy thing to do, Dad," he told Grandpa. "Your health's not good. And somebody could've gotten hurt!"

"But that's why I had to go with them, son. I knew I couldn't talk them out of it. So I thought it best to go with them in case there was trouble." He winked at me. "Anyway, I've never felt better or stronger in my life," he finished proudly.

"We couldn't have done it without you, Grandpa," I admitted. "There's no way we could've handled those buffalo alone."

"Frankly, I wasn't sure we could really do it," Grandpa confessed. "But I didn't want to spoil it for the kids."

Just then a loud laugh rang out from inside the house. They looked inside to see the tribal chairman standing in the midst of a circle of people. He was spinning a tall tale.

Robert shook his head. "Politicians. You can't do anything with 'em, and you can't do anything without 'em. Funny how the tribal chairman turned this into a political victory for himself," he said.

The three generations of men laughed and went back inside for dessert.

Chapter 12
Worthy of Being Cheyenne

It was decided that a naming ceremony would be held for me in honor of my daring act. Labor Day weekend was chosen for the event. At this ceremony, a medicine man chosen by Grandpa would give me an Indian name. Several traditional families of the tribe came together to sponsor the event.

When the time came, a circle of tipis was put up in the field next to the tribal community center. People from all over the reservation gathered there.

My mother and stepfather came to Buffalo Gap too. They were both very proud of me. I was excited and a little nervous about the whole thing.

The night before the ceremony, my extended family and I gathered in the center of the circle of tipis. Robert led us into the largest tipi.

An elderly Indian man with a wrinkled face was waiting for us inside. He was seated on a blanket in the back of the tipi. In front of him was a smaller blanket with several objects spread out on it. We all sat down in front of him. Robert introduced the man to us.

"This is Thomas Red Elk. He's the most respected holy man of our tribe. We are asking him to perform this ceremony for our family.

Red Elk nodded his head. Then Robert brought me to the front of the group.

"This is Danny," Robert said. "We are here to ask you to give him his Indian name." Robert pulled a pouch of tobacco out of his pocket and handed it to Red Elk. This is the traditional way of asking a medicine man to do anything.

"This is an honor for me," the old man said. "I am happy to do this for your family. It is good to carry on our traditions in this way. Your ancestors will be pleased." He put the tobacco down in front of him next to a beaded feather fan.

"Tomorrow at noon we will come together here in the circle of lodges," Red Elk said. "I'll ask the Creator to bless this boy for what he did for the good of his people. Then I'll ask for a blessing on our tribe."

He picked up a long leather pouch with fringes and beads and cradled it in the crook of his arm.

"Then we will come back here to smoke this sacred pipe. Each of you can speak what's in your mind and heart for the Creator to hear."

He put the pipe back down and picked up a small pouch. He untied the leather string, opened the pouch, and removed a pinch of its contents.

"Then I'm gonna smoke Danny with this cedar and this sage and give him his Indian name. After that comes my favorite part of the ritual—the food!"

He smiled a big grin. A few of his teeth were missing. "We'll have a thanksgiving meal and feed all these people who have come to witness this blessing."

The holy man stood up and walked over to me.

"Then we'll go over to the powwow grounds. The drum will start and we'll dance until midnight. How does this sound to you, Danny? Okay?"

"Yes, okay, I guess," I said. I was worried I wouldn't know what I was supposed to do or when.

"Don't worry. I'll tell you what to do, where to stand, and what to say. Everything will be fine. Just leave it to me."

I relaxed. Red Elk walked back to his blanket and sat down.

"Now leave me. I must prepare for tomorrow's activities. Go home and get a good night's sleep."

He shooed us away with a gesture of his hand.

The next morning, everyone at the Wind house was up early. Amanda and Grandma fixed a big breakfast that the family wolfed down in record time.

When I got out of the shower, I wrapped a towel around myself and went into my room to get dressed. My stepdad was there waiting for me.

"Danny, I just want you to know how proud I am of you," he said. "You took a lot of risks this summer and learned a lot about your own strengths."

He handed me a sack. I opened it and found a pair of beaded moccasins, brand new.

"Wow!" I said.

"I thought you might want to wear them today at the ceremony."

I took them out of the bag and looked at them. "Thanks! These are actually very cool." We were silent for an awkward moment.

"Well, I guess you'd better get ready," Bill said as he stood to leave.

"I'm sorry I've been such a problem," I said.

"It's okay," Bill replied. "You've been through some hard stuff. I think things will be better now." He smiled and left.

I put on my new pair of blue jeans and slipped on the moccasins.

Just then Aunt Amanda came in carrying something. "I made this for you to wear today at the ceremony," she said. She held up a bright yellow shirt with red and green ribbons on it. "It's a traditional man's ribbon shirt."

"It's awesome," I told her.

"I made one just like it for Robert to wear on our wedding day," she added. "Here, let me help you put it on." She slipped it on over my head. I looked at myself in the mirror.

Then Mom stuck her head in the door.

"You look very handsome, son," she said and stepped into the room.

"I've got something to round out your wardrobe for today." She held up a multicolored yarn belt. "I made it for you in the car while we were driving here."

She threaded the belt through the belt loops on my jeans and tied it in front.

"Now the look is complete," she said. "When you're all done, come into the kitchen and I'll braid your hair."

All the attention made me blush.

"Okay, everybody out," I said. "A fella needs a little privacy when he's dressing." Amanda and Mom looked at each other and winked.

"All right," Mom said. "Come on, Amanda. Let's give the man some space."

Later, the whole family gathered in the front yard so that Bill could take a group portrait. Everyone wore their best Indian clothes, except Bill. He stuck out like a sore thumb in his city clothes and bolo tie.

Bill set a camera up on a tripod. Then he arranged the family in three rows for the three generations. He went back to the camera and set the timer. Then he ran back to join the family. Everyone smiled and the camera flashed.

"There's one for your family photo album," Bill said to Mom.

We left for the ceremony and arrived at the tipi camp just before noon. I couldn't believe it. Hundreds of tribal people had gathered. I kind of got choked up for a minute. They were all there to see me.

Adults were setting up their folding chairs on the outer rim of the circle. Children were running and playing around the outside of the tipis.

On one side there were several chairs set up for invited guests. The tribal chairman was there, along with Park Ranger Perkins, a few tribal council members, and Martin Two Bulls.

Uncle Robert led the family to the front of the medicine man's tipi. We waited there for the ceremony to begin. I looked around the crowd and saw Ben and the other kids. Charlene was there too. She waved to me. I smiled and waved back.

A few minutes past noon, Thomas Red Elk came out of his tipi. He was dressed in buckskin, moccasins, headdress, and a large beaded belt.

He spoke to the crowd. "Today we are here to recognize and honor the deeds of one young man. He is a member of this nation and has brought honor to us. He will receive his Indian name, as is the way of our people."

Standing in front of Red Elk's tipi, we went through all the steps the old man had described the night before. The crowd waited quietly. Then, when the ceremony was completed, the medicine man spoke to the crowd.

"Daniel Nathan Wind came to us at the beginning of the summer as a confused boy. He didn't know himself or his people. Today I present to you a young man who has proven himself worthy of being called a Cheyenne and all that it means. I have given him a very old name, one that has not been used among our people for generations. From this day forth he shall be known as Buffalo Bringer."

The crowd applauded loud and long. Shouts of "Aho" could be heard. Grandpa had told me this means they approve of what's happening.

The medicine man took me to the center of the circle and told me to say something. I looked around at the large crowd. I'd never been the center of attention like this. I spotted Charlene and my friends again.

"I can't stand here alone and take all the credit for bringing the buffalo back. The truth is, I wouldn't have been able to do any of it without a whole circle of family and friends doing their part, too. So I want my family and my friends to come up here with me."

They all gathered around me. Charlene moved up next to me and clasped my hand. She had a big silly grin on her face. I blushed again. Then I took a deep breath and let it out.

"I also realized that being Cheyenne means that I am connected to the earth," I continued. "I'm connected to my animal brothers and to all of you. None of us is ever alone. I say thank you to all my relations." The audience applauded again.

"Hoka!" Thomas Red Elk shouted. "Now let's eat!"

The old man led the way toward the community center. There a feast of Native American foods had been prepared and laid out. I stood with Charlene as the rest of my family headed for the food.

"I'll catch up to you in a minute," I told Mom. I took a deep breath and let it out.

"Charlene, you're a nice girl. And you're pretty and all." What was I going to say next?

"But I have to go back to L.A. soon. I'm not ready for a girlfriend or anything yet."

She frowned and turned away. "I thought you liked me," she said.

"I do. Believe me, I do. But can we just be friends for now? I promise I'll write and tell you what I'm doing. And you can write and tell me what's going on here on the rez."

She thought about it for a minute, and then turned back to me.

"Okay," she said with a smile. Everything was suddenly all right.

"But just you wait two or three years, Daniel Nathan Wind—I mean, Buffalo Bringer," she said with a gleam in her eye. "Then we'll see who wants to just be friends."

She laughed and we went to eat. I let out a big sigh of relief. Talking to a girl was much harder than driving a herd of buffalo across the plains.

The powwow began in the middle of the afternoon. Grandma had made a Straight Dance outfit for me to wear. Grandpa, Robert, and I went into the men's restroom and changed into our outfits. Amanda, Mom, and Grandma dressed in the ladies' room.

As Grandpa, Uncle, and I left the dressing room, Robert stopped me to straighten part of my outfit.

"You look just right," Robert said. He put his hand on my shoulder. "I know your father is watching you today from the spirit world. He's proud of you. You've come a long way, nephew, but don't stop now. Keep growing the way you're growing. You'll be a fine man one day, a Cheyenne man." He patted me on the back. Then we walked toward the sound of the drum.

When everyone in the family was ready, we entered the powwow arena together. The drum group, seated in the middle, began an honor song for the family. The arena director led me into the arena first. I circled the drum alone once. Then Grandpa and Uncle stepped in beside me, continuing around the circle.

Then Mom and Bill fell in behind us. The rest of the family and my friends from summer survival camp joined in. Finally, others in the crowd joined the circling dancers. A large mass of people circled the drum as the singers pounded out the song. It echoed across the fields.

At sunset, layers of blue, pink, and orange clouds gathered on the horizon. And while the singers sang and the dancers danced, a small circle of dust floated outside the circle.

I looked closer at the floating dust. I thought I could see the wispy shapes of buffalo dancing around the outer edge of the circle.

"Grandpa!" I shouted.

"Yes, Danny, I see them. The buffalo spirits. They've come to honor you, too. I told you—they're proud to be with us once more."

I looked again. Among the buffalo spirits there, I swore I saw my father's spirit dancing with us.

And he smiled.

About the Author

Gary Robinson, a writer and filmmaker of Cherokee and Choctaw Indian descent, has spent more than twenty-five years working with American Indian communities to tell the historical and contemporary stories of Native people in all forms of media. His television work has aired on PBS, Turner Broadcasting, Ovation Network, and others. His nonfiction books, *From Warriors to Soldiers* and *The Language of Victory*, reveal little-known aspects of American Indian service in the U.S. military from the Revolutionary War to modern times. In addition to *Thunder on the Plains*, he has written another novel, *Tribal Journey*, and two children's books that share aspects of Native American culture through popular holiday themes: *Native American Night Before Christmas* and *Native American Twelve Days of Christmas*. He lives in rural central California.

7th Generation *publications celebrate the stories and achievements of Native people in North America through fiction and biography.*

For more information, visit:
nativevoicesbooks.com

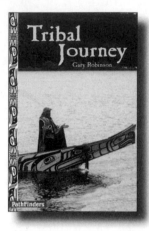

Tribal Journey
Gary Robinson
978-1-939053-01-5
$9.95

A young Native teen is forced to deal with becoming partially paralyzed as the result of a car accident caused when both drivers were texting. Jason's lucky to be alive—but life in a wheelchair seems too much to bear. Even when he was protecting his mom and siblings from his drunken father, or escaping from home to be with his friends, he never imagined something like this could happen to him.

Now Jason sees himself only as a kid who will always be paralyzed. But when he becomes part of the Raven Canoe Family and learns to "pull" a canoe, his outlook on life begins to change. After completing a two-week tribal canoe journey with his Duwamish tribal members, Jason is proud to be a Coast Salish Indian. From the hardships and camaraderie of the journey, he gains a new sense of courage and determination to someday swim and walk again.